A ROYAL Wedding

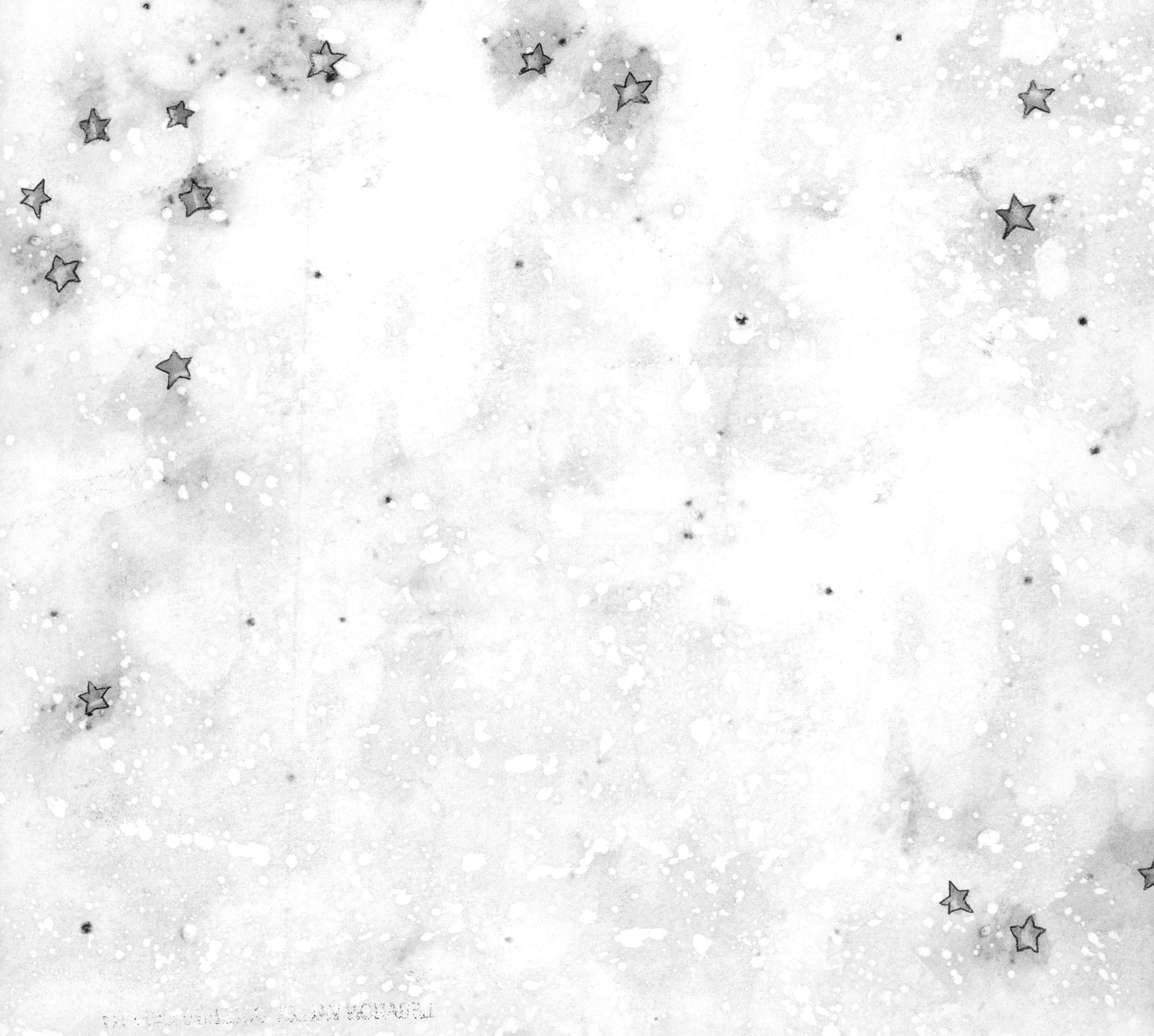

A ROYAL Wedding

Written by
Mark Kimball Moulton
Art by
Karen Hillard Good

RIVERTON PRESS

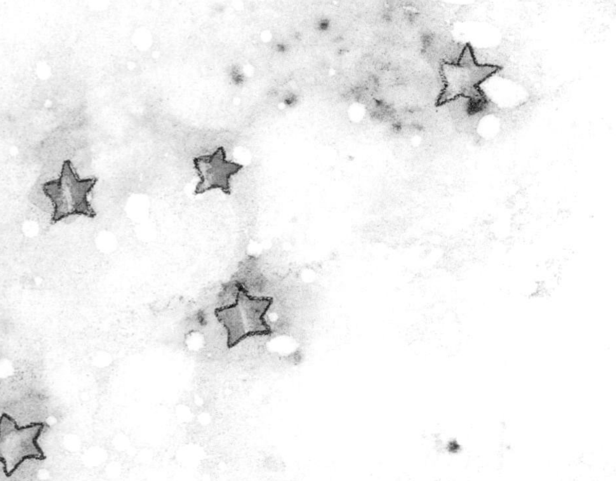

ISBN-13: 978-0-8249-8677-3
ISBN-10: 0-8249-8677-6

Published by Riverton Press

Distributed by Ideals Publications
A Guideposts Company
535 Metroplex Drive, Suite 250
Nashville, Tennessee 37211
www.idealspublications.com

Color separations by Precision Color Graphics, Franklin, Wisconsin

Printed and bound in Italy by LEGO

Library of Congress Cataloging-in-Publication data on file

10 9 8 7 6 5 4 3 2 1

Designed by Georgina Chidlow-Rucker

Proudly presented to:
From:
Date:

Not far away,
just beyond the sunrise,
is a land ruled by spiders
and blue bottle flies,

where mosquitoes laugh
and dragonflies giggle
at jokes told by turtles
and worms as they wiggle.

It's a wonderful place filled
with beauty and grace,
where life is lived slowly,
**just at a
snail's pace.**

So open the window and follow your dreams
out through the brown fields, down the path by the stream.
Find a comfortable seat lit by a moonbeam
and hear this tale of Fieldmouse and his beloved Queen.

(It's a tale of the most enchanting romance,
that began at the Annual Midsummer Eve Dance.)

Please join us for our
Annual
Midsummer Eve Dance.
There will be music
and cake
and a bit of romance.

Dear Queen Spider was
weaving a web for her bed
when Sir Fieldmouse came calling.
He bowed and he said,

"Time has come,
my dear Queen,
for your work
to be done.

"You've toiled all the day
and your web's nearly spun.

"May I ask you to join me
in a dance, just for fun?"

Well, Queen Spider, she stuttered,
she blushed, and she cried.
For a date with Sir Fieldmouse,
any girl would have died!

"Why yes, my good Fieldmouse,
I'd love to attend,
and dance till my eight legs
will no longer bend.

"After all, it is evening and
my work now should end~
but you must call me 'Queenie'
if we're to be friends."

So the Royal Flea-Maidens
helped Queenie to don
a shimmering gown
of the softest
chiffon.

Fieldmouse brought gardenias
and chocolate bonbons.
He looked oh, so regal
with his tuxedo on.

They enlisted a firefly
and flew to the ball~
Queen Spider held tight
so that neither would fall.

They arrived with a flourish,
long before curtain call,
and they bowed and they curtsied
to one
and to all.

They made quite the entrance;
their friends were so pleased.
"What have we here,
a new couple?"
they teased.
But Queenie and Mouse
paid no attention to these.

This enchanting affair
was held on the banks of
Swan Lake.

There were cattails with candles
and a juicy clam bake and
dandelion puffs

that blew through the air with
each shake
and drinks chilled with
glistening, tiny snowflakes;
and at midnight they served
a magnificent cake.

The orchestra struck up
a soft "Pastorale,"
then crooned out a love song
called "Me and My Gal."

Cricket played the viola,
Moth her violin.
Toad croaked out the chorus,
Tree Frog joined right in.

Madam Bee of the Bumble
hummed a beautiful tune,
and a romantic ballad
was sung by Miss Loon.

"and a one
and a two..."
"You are my
Sunshine..."

The First Lady Bug flirted
and batted her eyes
at the handsome
Little Lord Blue Bottlefly.

That he flirted back
was no big surprise,
for the First Lady's beauty
was well recognized.

Butterfly had arrived
from the Castle Cocoon~
she was recently back from
her long honeymoon.

She flew on the dance floor
with grace and finesse,
and she swirled and she twirled
in her long, flowing dress.

Reverend Mantis was praying
and said just a word
'bout the dee-licious dinner
that soon would be served.

There was dandelion salad
and roast chestnut pâtè,
and, in honor of Queenie,
bowls of fresh curds and whey.

Caterpillar sailed in
on a leaf for his boat
to show off his fluffy, new,
striped winter coat.

He hadn't a penny
to pay for his meal,
so he did a tap dance that made
everyone squeal.

reserved
for
Queenie
"Thank
You for
this food,
Amen."
"Wow!"

By eleven the party was still going quite strong.

Queenie and Sir Fieldmouse had danced every song,
and Queen Spider's eight legs had kept up all night long.

They dazzled the crowd, they made quite the pair,
with the moon in their eyes and starlight in their hair.

Soon Queenie was smitten and Sir Fieldmouse, in love.
Their friends were so happy that's all they talked of!

Months later, Sir Fieldmouse
bent down on one knee,
feeling shy and as nervous
as nervous can be, and he asked,
"My dear Queenie,
will you please
marry me?"
Once again, Queenie Spider
blushed, stuttered, and cried~
she was thrilled though
she acted demure
and surprised;
and she teased him by keeping
her feelings disguised.
Then she giggled,
"Why yes, dear.
I shall be
your bride!"

"What a lovely wedding!"
"Do you promise to Love each other?"
"Ah... Amore."

Their wedding was royal,
a majestic affair,
no wedding before could
come close or compare~

anyone who was "someone"
was certainly there.
Now our Queenie and Fieldmouse
are happy, they say,
though he works late at night
and she weaves in the day.

For they're loved and respected
by all that they meet,
and their love for each other
has made them complete.
And a love such as that
is a hard love to beat.

But still why, you might ask,
would a mouse love a bug?
Think of Queenie's eight legs

and how she must hug!

And though they are different
in station and form,
and some folks might say
they don't fully conform,
their lives are just perfect,
though far from the norm~
he keeps her in bonbons,
her hugs keep him warm.

**And isn't that
what love's
really all about?**

"Your eyes outshine the stars."
Love Poems
"We're so cute."

Just married